Starry Night, Hold Me Tight

by Jean Sagendorph
Illustrated by Kim Siebold

RP|KIDS
PHILADELPHIA • LONDON

Printed in China

Books published by Running Press are available at special discounts for bulk purchases in the United States by corporations, institutions, and other organizations. For more information, please contact the Special Markets Department at the Perseus Books Group, 2300 Chestnut Street, Suite 200, Philadelphia, PA 19103, or call (800) 810-4145, ext. 5000, or e-mail special.markets@perseusbooks.com.

ISBN 978-0-7624-4066-5
Library of Congress Control Number: 2010935842

9 8 7 6 5 4 3 2 1
Digit on the right indicates the number of this printing

Cover and interior design by Frances J. Soo Ping Chow
Edited by Marlo Scrimizzi
Typography: Brownstone and La Portentia

Published by Running Press Kids
an imprint of Running Press Book Publishers
A Member of the Perseus Books Group
2300 Chestnut Street
Philadelphia, PA 19103-4371

Visit us on the web!
www.runningpress.com

For Sam

—JS

To my little inspirations . . .

Kayla, Haley, Hunter, and Jake

—KS

Starry night, hold me tight.

All is calm, all is bright.

Big bear hugs, morning, noon, and night.
Momma's love helps Baby
soar like a kite.

Adventures will help Baby Bear
learn and grow.
Even when he plays in the snow.

All the baby bears love to slide!
All the mommas watch
with pride.

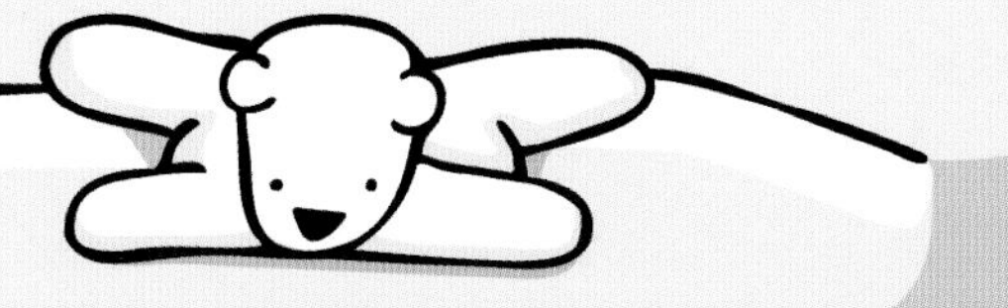

Momma's fur is soft and warm
Keeping Baby safe in the big snowstorm.

Baby Bear loves to make angels
in the fallen snow.
On the most perfect one, Baby will place a bow.

Momma Bear teaches many things to Baby Bear.
Today's lesson: to be a good friend,
one must share.

Baby Bear loves a good snowball fight!

Don't throw one at Momma.

It's not polite.

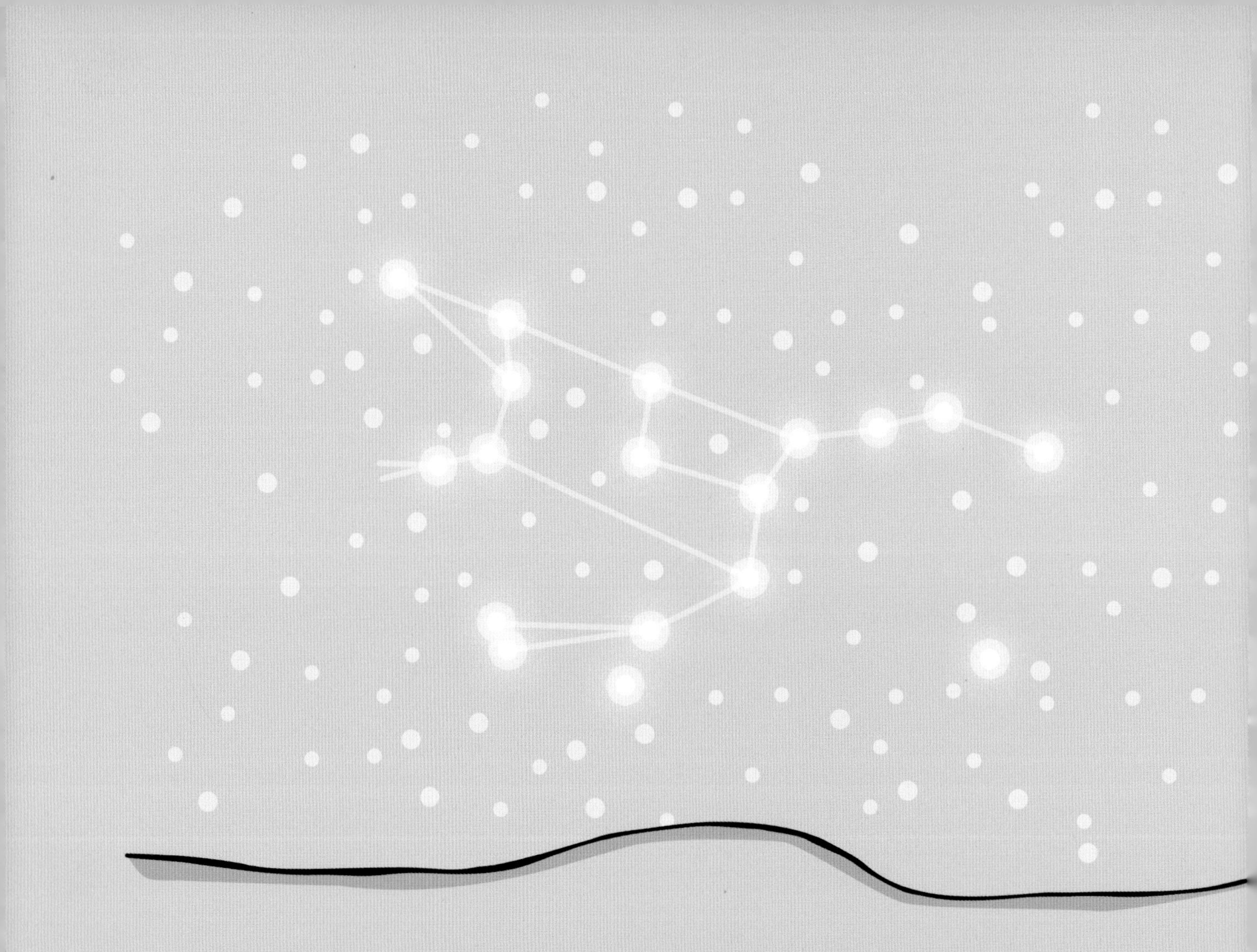

Momma points to the Great Bear in the sky.

Twinkling stars are up so high!

When Baby Bear puts away his toys,
Momma Bear is filled with lots of joy.

Late at night, all warm in his den,
Baby Bear says his prayers, amen.

Sleepy cub lulled by Momma’s song.
Morning will come soon;
it won’t be long.

Sleep in heavenly peace,

is Momma's prayer.

Sleep in heavenly peace, little Baby Bear.

Goodnight.